W9-AHR-332

The Snow Party

BY BEATRICE SCHENK DE REGNIERS
DRAWINGS BY REINER ZIMNIK

PANTHEON BOOKS

There was this little old woman and this little old man and they lived in a little old farmhouse 'way out in Dakota.

They lived all alone on the farm with some chickens.

Outside it was snowing and snowing and the wind was
blowing.

And the little old woman said, "I'm mighty lonely here with
just you and the chickens for company. I'd like to give me a
party and have plenty of folks in."

And the little old man said, "What's the matter with you, woman? Are you daft? We don't know a soul to invite to a party.

"And if we did know a soul, who would come to a party through all this wind and snow?"

The little old woman looked out of the window and she could see that outside it was snowing and snowing. And she could hear the wind blowing.

And she said, "I'd bake me a cake and put candles on it and I'd hire me a fiddler to fiddle a tune and there would be feasting and dancing and merry-making. There would be high jinks and low jinks. It would be a fine party, I can tell you."

"Woman, are you daft?" said the little old man. "Even if we knew a soul to invite to a party and even if they came through the wind and the snow, we don't have a crust or a crumb of cake or a thimbleful of flour in the house to bake one."

Outside it was snowing and snowing and the wind was blowing.

Inside, the little old woman turned on all the lights so the house wouldn't look so lonely. And she turned on the radio so the house wouldn't sound so lonely.

The man on the radio was advertising the K-M Bakery. He was saying, "The next time you have a party, order K-M's luscious, delicious, delightful, and simply heavenly chocolate fudge cake. And remember, the K-M Bakery delivers its delicious cakes, bread, pies, cupcakes, cinnamon rolls, and buns right to your door. So . . .

> when you hear that
> knock-knock
> knock-knock-knock
> answer the door as fast as you can, 'cause
> knock-knock
> knock-knock-knock
> means here comes the K-M man!"

"Chocolate cake," the little old woman sighed. "Cinnamon rolls, buns . . ."

Then all of a sudden the wind blew hard and harder and it blew down the electric lines and the radio went off and the lights went out and it was dark in the little house.

So the little old woman lit candles. She had a lot of candles and she lit them all and put them on the table.

The table looked like a big birthday cake, it had so many candles all around it.

"I wish it were a cake," said the little old woman. "I wish the table were a big cake and we were having a party."

"Hush, woman," said the little old man. "Wishes won't wash dishes and wishes won't stop the wind from blowing or the snow from snowing." And he put on his high galoshes

and his overcoat and his hat and his earmuffs and his mittens.

"Where are you going in all this snow and wind?" asked the little old woman.

"We have 300 baby chicks in the barn and I'm going to bring them into the house to keep them warm. Three hundred chirping chicks will be company enough."

"Well, bring in the chicks," said the little old woman, "but that's not the company I'm wishing for."

And the little old man went out the back door to the barn with the snow snowing and the wind blowing.

Listen!

There is a knock at the front door—knock-knock!

The little old woman hurries to the door. "Who could be knocking at our door," she says, "on a night like this with the snow snowing and the wind blowing."

She opens the door and in comes a great blast of wind and snow and there stands a man saying, "My car is stuck in the snow with a carload of people. Would you be good enough, old woman, to let us come in out of the snow and the wind until the snow plow comes to clear the road?"

"Come in, come in," says the little old woman, "and bring your carload of people and welcome!" And she scoops up a panful of snow and puts it on the stove to boil to make a pot of hot tea.

The man goes to his car and brings back his wife and his mother and his three brothers-in-law. And his wife is carrying a tiny baby wrapped in a blanket.

The little old man is bringing in a basket full of chirping chicks. He says, "Welcome, welcome. Make yourselves at home. My little old woman was wishing for company."

Then he picks up a box and goes out the back door again to bring in some more baby chicks.

Listen!

There is a knock at the front door—knock-knock!

The little old woman hurries to the door and there in the wind and the snow stand a man and his wife and their twin boys and another man and a big hunting dog.

Their car is stuck in the snow and they are waiting for the snow plow to come through and clear the road.

"Come in, come in," says the little old woman, "and welcome! There's plenty of hot tea to drink, though there's not a crust or a crumb of cake or bread in the house to eat with it."

Then the little old man comes in with a box full of chirping chicks. Now there are 11 grownups and 1 baby and 2 little boys and a big hunting dog in the house.

"Welcome, welcome," says the little old man. "My little old woman was wishing for company and now she has it." And once again he goes out the back door and into the wind and snow to bring in some more baby chicks.

Outside the snow is snowing and the wind is blowing and the strangers are glad to be inside.

But listen!

Someone is knocking at the front door—knock-knock!

The little old woman hurries to the door and there are three carloads of people. Their cars are stuck in the snow and they must wait for the snow plow to come through to clear the road.

"Come in, come in," says the little old woman, "and welcome!"

So now when the little old man comes in the back door with a box of chirping baby chicks, he counts 27 grownups, 5 children, 3 babies, 2 dogs, and a parakeet.

All night long people come knocking at the door.

Now there are 84 grownups, 17 children, 7 babies, 6 dogs, a cat, a parakeet, a canary bird, and a little pet skunk in the little old house.

Outside it is snowing and snowing and the wind is blowing.

Inside, the babies are yowling, the dogs are yapping, the chicks are chirping, the mothers are scolding.

"It's a shame," says the little old woman, "it's a shame. All these people and no party. If only there were a crust or a crumb of cake or bread in the house or a bit of music."

But listen!

Someone is knocking at the door. It is a very special knock—

> knock-knock
>
> knock-knock-knock
>
> knock-knock
>
> knock-knock-knock

The little old woman hurries to open the door.

It is the K-M
man, the man from the K-M Bakery. His trailer truck is stuck
in the snow right in front of the door.

"Come in, come in," says the little old woman, "and welcome."

The K-M man comes in and he looks around at all the people
there and he says, "You look like mighty hungry people to me."

And the little old woman says, "There's not a crust or a crumb
of bread or cake in the house, but you're welcome to come in out
of the wind and the snow."

"Who will help me," says the K-M man. "Who will help me unload my truck?" Then he chooses some of the children and some of the grownup men.

What a parade!

First come the trays full of rolls—crunchy crusty rolls, brown and shiny; soft fluffy rolls, white and powdery; poppyseed rolls, sesame seed rolls, little rolls braided like ribbons, smooth round rolls shaped like a baby's bottom.

Then come the trays of cinnamon buns. The cinnamon makes the air smell like perfume.

Now comes a special parade of pies—lemon meringue pies, cherry pies, apple pies, coconut custard pies, chocolate cream pies.

Now come the cupcakes—chocolate, vanilla—with pink icing, white icing, rich chocolate icing.

The little old woman jumps up and down and claps her hands. "It's a party," she says. "It's a party sure enough."

"Ha," says the K-M man, "if it's a party, I'd better bring in my special-order chocolate fudge party cake."

So he brings it in and the little old woman puts candles all around it and somebody makes party hats out of newspapers and everyone eats to his heart's content.

Then the accordion player plays his accordion and he plays so gaily that no one can sit still. Everyone stamps his feet to the music. Even the babies wave their fat little hands and feet in time to the music.

Now the accordion player plays a waltz tune and the little old man grabs the little old woman around the waist and waltzes with her till they are both out of breath (which doesn't take very long) and everybody claps hands and begins to dance too.

The accordion player plays and plays. He plays "Turkey in the Hay, Turkey in the Straw" and he plays "Pop Goes the Weasel" and he plays "I Put My Left Foot In"—oh, he knows a hundred tunes and he plays them all!

It's a party, all right. There is feasting and dancing and merrymaking. There are high jinks and low jinks. It's a fine party, I can tell you.

The party lasts until noontime—when the snow stops snowing and the wind stops blowing and the snow plows come through and clear the road.

Everyone says goodbye to the little old woman and the little old man and they all say it is the best party they have ever been to.

The little old woman is so content and so happy and so tired and so sleepy that she lays her head on the table next to a coconut custard pie and falls fast asleep . . .

. . . and dreams about the party all over again.

End